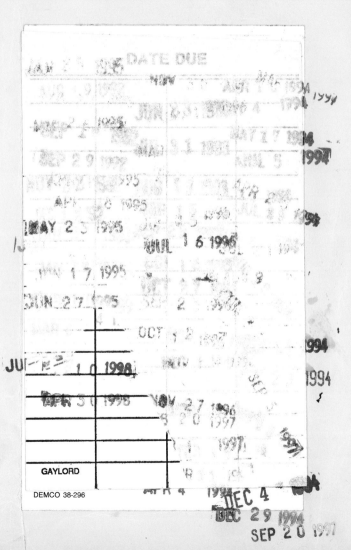

AN ORDINARY CAT

AN ORDINARY CAT

Story and Pictures by Christine Kettner

HarperCollins*Publishers*

Library of Congress Cataloging-in-Publication Data

Kettner, Christine.
  An ordinary cat / story and pictures by Christine Kettner.
      p.   cm.
  Summary: Everyone thinks William is an ordinary cat, but every
night he goes into town and does extraordinary things.
  ISBN 0-06-023172-6. — ISBN 0-06-023173-4 (lib. bdg.)
    [1. Cats—Fiction.] I. Title.
PZ7.K495Or 1991   90-19441
[E]—dc20   CIP
                                            AC

For Stephen

Everybody thinks William is an ordinary cat,

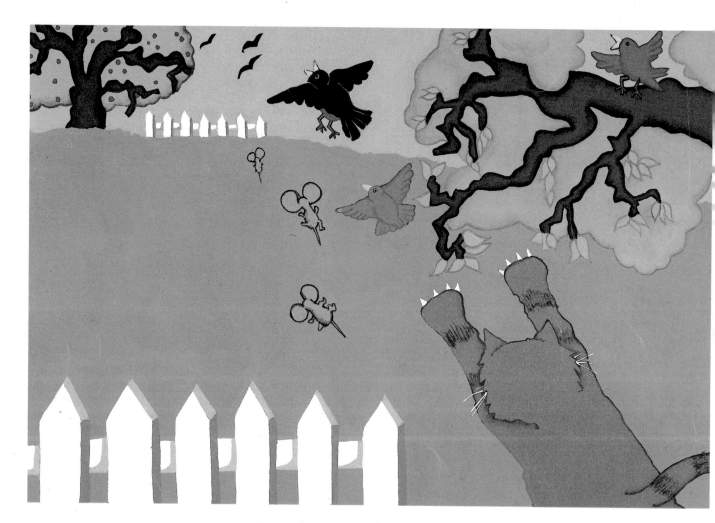

who does ordinary things.

But William is not like other cats.

Every night he slips quietly out his front door.

He turns right at the oak tree, skips past the mailbox, walks over the hill, and heads straight into town.

William greets his friends on his way to work.

Then he jumps into his taxi cab.

He picks up Felicia Flamingo, who is always late. William gets her to where she is going in the nick of time.

Sophie Squirrel is hard to please, but William knows where she can get the best bargain in town.

When he drives Mayor Bear to important meetings, William always gives her good advice.

He helps officer Howard Hound catch robbers and outlaws.

And when Clara Crab is feeling blue, William knows how to cheer her up.

After work, William always has his nails sharpened at Peggy Pig's
Beauty Shop because...

every night he plays banjo with his friends

at the Meow-Bow-Wow.

But every morning before the sun rises,

William walks back over the hill, past the mailbox, and left at the oak tree

to his place by the window,

to his milk in a bowl,

to behaving nicely for company,

to sneaking up on mice and birds,

to the family that loves him,

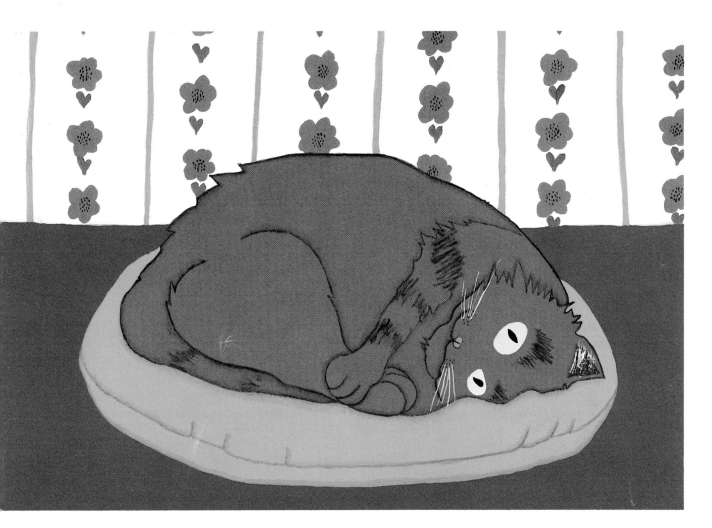

and to the ordinary ways

of an ordinary cat.